For our favorite readers . . .

Peter, Rachel, and Jordan
Love, Grandma Sue

Dakota, Molly, Steven, Alex, Nathaniel,
Joey, Matthew, and Nicholas
Love, Grammy

and to
Carol Lloyd . . .
lovely librarian and friend
—D & S

To my brother Thomas
—M.G.

Text copyright © 2008 by Debbie Bertram and Susan Bloom
Illustrations copyright © 2008 by Michael Garland
All rights reserved.
Published in the United States by Random House Children's Books, a division of Random House, Inc., New York.
Random House and colophon are registered trademarks of Random House, Inc.
Visit us on the Web! www.randomhouse.com/kids
Educators and librarians, for a variety of teaching tools, visit us at www.randomhouse.com/teachers

Library of Congress Cataloging-in-Publication Data
Bertram, Debbie.
The best book to read / by Debbie Bertram & Susan Bloom ; illustrated by Michael Garland. — 1st ed.
p. cm.
Summary: A young boy goes to the library with his class
and hears about the many kinds of books that can be found there.
ISBN 978-0-375-84702-8 (trade) — ISBN 978-0-375-94702-5 (lib. bdg.)
[1. Libraries—Fiction. 2. Books and reading—Fiction. 3. School field trips—Fiction. 4. Stories in rhyme.]
I. Bloom, Susan (Susan Lynn). II. Garland, Michael, ill. III. Title.
PZ8.3.B4595Bb 2008   [E]—dc22   2007026716

MANUFACTURED IN MALAYSIA
10 9 8 7 6 5 4 3 2 1
First Edition

The
Best Book to Read

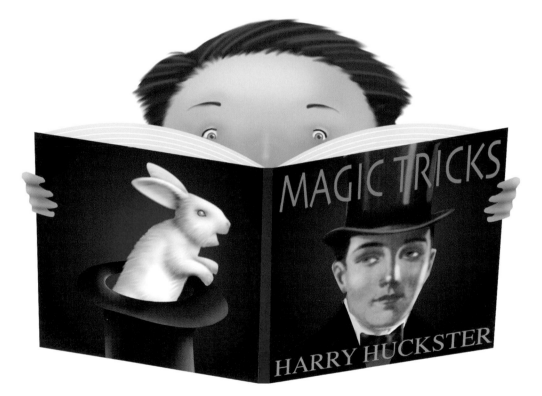

MAGIC TRICKS

HARRY HUCKSTER

by Debbie Bertram & Susan Bloom illustrated by Michael Garland

Random House New York

Hooray! It's a trip to the library today.
We line up as we get off the bus.
We've been specially invited. Our class is excited!
The librarian is welcoming us.

"Hello, boys and girls," the librarian says.
"I see faces I've seen here before.
Finding books can be fun!
You may choose more than one.
And my job is to help you explore—

Picture books, chapter books, books that pop up,
nonfiction, and fairy tales, too.
You may look by yourselves.
Take some books from the shelves.
Then check out the best book for you."

"With this outer-space book, it's time to lift off.
Three, two, one . . . now we blast off to Mars!
It's fun to pretend you're in space with a friend
as your rocket ship zooms toward the stars."

"A fire-breathing dragon comes alive in this book.
The princess and prince must be ready.
They will fight night and day,
keeping hot flames away,
on guard with their shields and swords steady."

"Entomology is the study of bugs.
Read this book, learn how many there are.
Collect bugs with great care,
punching holes for some air
in the lid of an old pickle jar."

"Dessert, anyone? Here's a recipe book.
Pour sugar, mix butter, add flour.
Now you're ready to bake
a big fudge birthday cake.
Lick the bowl and then frost in one hour."

"Read a dinosaur book that goes way back in time.
Pterodactyls are hunting for prey.
T. rex, on the prowl,
roars a big hungry GROWL.
Frightened raptors are running away."

"Who has a dog?" the librarian asks.
"Here's a book about being a trainer.
'Sit!' 'Stay!' and 'Play dead!'
'Do not jump on Mom's bed!'
Training dogs will become a no-brainer."

"*Abracadabra!* A magic-trick book.
Pull a quarter right out of your ear.
Wave your wand—just like that, rabbits jump from a hat!
Then—*presto!*—they all disappear."

"*I* want *that* book!"

"Me too!"

"So do I!"

"Doing magic would be so much fun."

"If you want the same book, then let's go take a look.
Very often we have more than one."

"Raise your hand if you want your own library card.
Sign your name on the line if you do.
With your new card in hand, your book will be scanned.
Bring it back by the date when it's due."

"Do you all have a book?" the librarian asks.
We hold up our books. "Yes!" we say.
"I see books about history, adventure, and mystery—
So many great choices today."

We climb back on the bus with our library books.
Lots of reading will help us succeed.
From page one to the end, a good book is a friend.
Now we *all* have the best book to read!

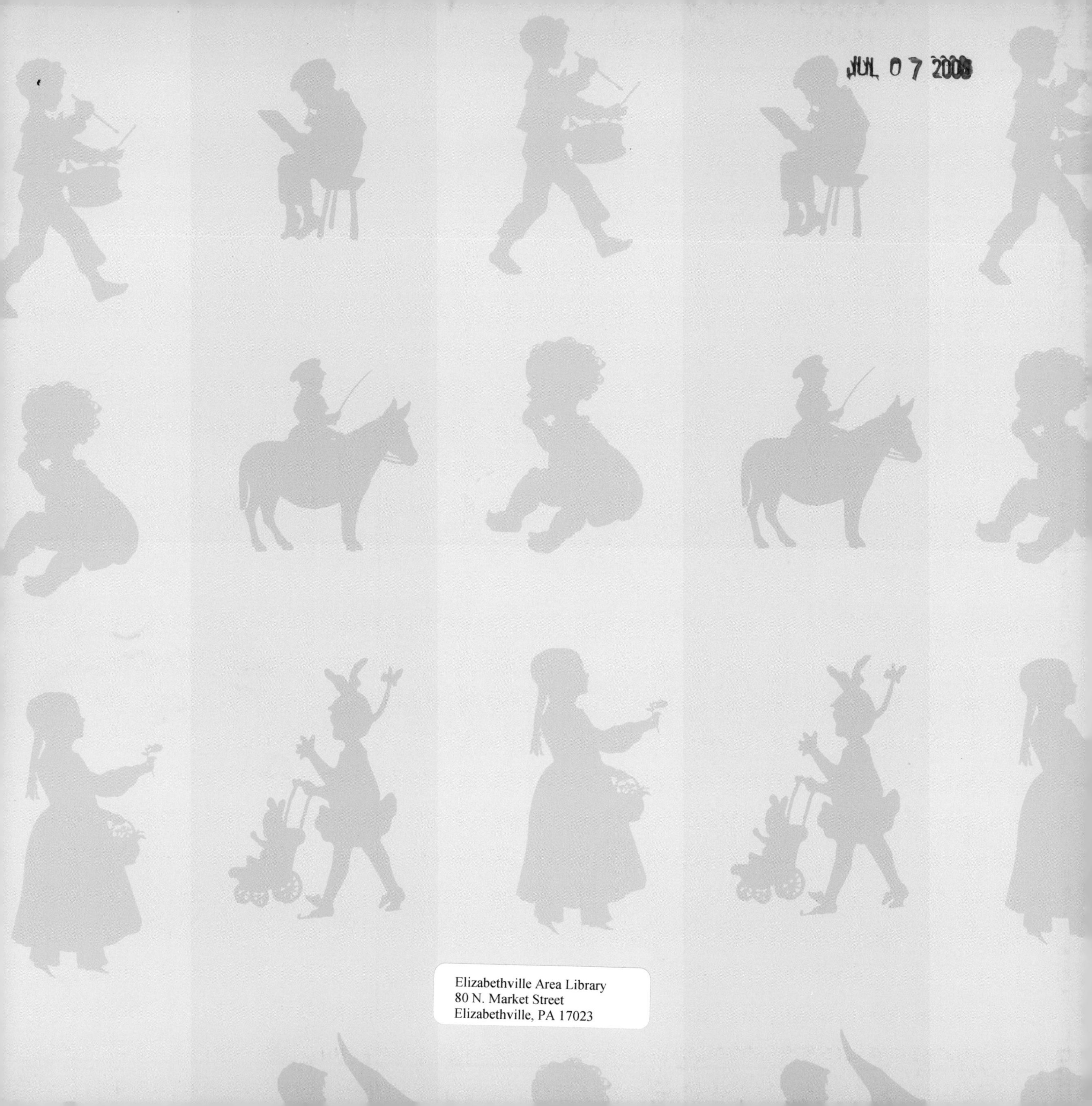